CW01220280

SEVEN DEAD SISTERS

SEVEN DEAD SISTERS

Jen Williams

SEVEN DEAD SISTERS
Copyright Jen Williams © 2022

Cover Art
Copyright Vince Haig © 2022

Introduction
Copyright Marie O'Regan © 2022

This hardcover edition is published in May 2022 by Absinthe Books, an imprint of PS Publishing Ltd, by arrangement with the author. All rights reserved by the author.

The right of Jen Williams to be identified as Author of this Work has been asserted by her in accordance with the Copyright, Designs & Patents Act 1988.

This book is a work of fiction. Names, characters, places and incidents either are products of the author's imagination or are used fictitiously. Any resemblance to actual events or locales or persons, living or dead, is entirely coincidental.

ISBN
978-1-78636-838-6
978-1-78636-837-9 (signed edition)

Design & Layout by Michael Smith
Printed and bound in England by TJ Books

ABSINTHE BOOKS
PS Publishing | Grosvenor House
1 New Road Hornsea, HU18 1PG | United Kingdom

editor@pspublishing.co.uk | www.pspublishing.co.uk

Introduction

I'VE LOVED JEN'S WRITING EVER SINCE HER FIRST novel, *The Copper Promise*, the first volume of the Copper Cat trilogy, and was delighted when she agreed to write a short story for our anthology, *Cursed*, from Titan Books. She is also the author of the Winnowing Flame trilogy, and her first crime novel, *Dog Rose Dirt*, is released this year—and I already have it pre-ordered.

With *Seven Dead Sisters*, you're in for a real treat. Alizon Grey is being driven to her death, caged in the back of a cart ready to be burned to death as a witch, and for killing her father. When the cart is attacked and she finds herself loose, we follow her journey as she tries to reach safety even as the story of her life—mistreated and the last of her siblings—is gradually revealed. Alizon has had to fight for her life before now, but this time wins all and the truth will be revealed.

—Marie O'Regan
Derbyshire, 2020

SEVEN DEAD SISTERS

*For anyone who ever asked the faeries for a boon . . .
we know who we are.*

Chapter One

THE FLOOR OF THE CART WAS STREWN WITH DIRTY straw, as though she were little more than a pig off to slaughter, which Alizon Grey thought was likely appropriate. Add insult to injury, why not? Around her, the iron bars that had been cunningly heated and beaten into a cage rose up, painting weak shadows across her feet in the chilly early morning light. She knocked her foot against the wooden planks and wondered if people pissed themselves on the way to their burning. It smelled like they did.

"You leave that off, Alizon Grey. You ought to be spending your last hours throwing yerself upon His mercy." At the head of the cart, the magistrate John Bowman turned and looked at her over his shoulder. He was a squat man with a wide mouth. Something of the frog about him, or toad. Alizon thought about putting him on a hot iron skillet and watching him go pop. "Least you can do is not give us trouble now. But I suppose those who have grown and sprouted in sin can no more change theirselves than a dog can become a man."

Fancies himself a poet. It's him who should be praying forgiveness for his hackneyed words.

"Cost you too much in kindling, have I, Master Bowman?" Alizon watched his face for a reaction, but he just glared at her and turned back. The driver of the cart was a man called Thomas Whittle, and he was a different sort of creature. He was tall and had hair so black his chin looked blue, and his lips were colourless. Alizon thought nothing of John Bowman, but she was wise enough to be scared of Thomas Whittle. He had not spoken since they had gotten her in the cart, but now his deep voice rumbled. He didn't trouble to turn away from his two horses.

"The flames will burn her pure again," he said. "She'll repent sure enough when the bottoms of her skirts start to smoke. They all do."

The rumour in the village was that Thomas Whittle travelled to see as many hangings and burnings as he could. That he scraped up the hot fat that was left after and touched it to his lips. Alizon turned away from them both and looked out at the passing world, one hand pressed to her stomach, which was starting to give her some discomfort.

This road was old, older than the village. It cut through the thickest part of the forest, hard dirt packed down and tamed into ragged brown lines, but the trees still pressed in on either side, a solid green presence. From here you followed the road to a fork, where you could take the road to the right and travel to Dyersbrook, a neighbouring village—or you took the road to the left and headed up an incline until the trees grew scarcer again and you got to Demdike Hill. Here was a ring of old stones, and here was the burning place. The killing road. Theirs was a wild and lawless country, remote from the king's eye and the church's heart, but men like John Bowman were happy to weave their own laws out of the threads of weakness and fear. Who would know, or care? Alizon's own family were all now dead and gone—she had made certain of that herself—and people who saw the flames dancing at the top of the hill would think they lit a beacon for midsummer, or some other reason. People were always lighting fires.

It was summer, and it was hot, but on the killing road the trees seemed to eat up the light and heat. Alizon wore the dress she'd been wearing when they came for her, and her feet were bare and dirty. Her hair was pushed inside a white cotton cap, and as the cart rumbled on she pulled the cap off, letting her brown hair—in need of a wash, truthfully—fall to her shoulders. In the trees, it looked briefly like something was moving beyond the trunks, keeping pace with the cart. Alizon blinked rapidly and the impression was lost.

"It goes up faster," said Thomas Whittle then. "If you leave your hair down, it'll catch like dry straw and crisp right off your head. I've seen it happen."

Alizon had not seen him turn and look at her. She turned the cap around in her hands, refusing to think about it, but Whittle continued.

"Every bit of pain you inflicted on your father will be cast tenfold on you, girl." He sounded almost wistful. "You will scream for forgiveness then. Mark it. I've seen it."

Alizon picked a piece of straw from her cap. When she had been around five or six years old, she had seen her father pluck the new baby from her mother's arms and take it outside to the goat's water bucket. Alizon had crept out after him and watched as he held the small thing upside down in the water. It did not move much. She had hoped that she would get to name this baby, had picked out a name in anticipation—Bethan—but in the end she had barely seen it before it was lost. Later, there was a new, darker patch of earth at the edge of their home, and no one in the village said anything. It was a lean year. Babies died in childbirth all the time.

When her mother's belly began to swell again, Alizon took a clay cup from the hearth and half-filled it with milk from the goat, and she left it out by the back door. She wanted a faerie protector, a spell to save a brother or a sister—like in the old stories. If they were in danger, they could turn into a deer and run away, or a bird that could fly up to where their father couldn't reach them. *Faerie Queen, protect my unborn brother or sister.* But instead, the milk was still there the next morning, frozen solid, and her father caught her by the arm and beat her until her body was cloudy with bruises. It is a sin to waste milk, he told her.

She thought of the old milk curdling in her mother's breasts and said nothing.

The men had lapsed into silence again, and as if the state were infectious, a greater quiet seemed to spread out through the wood. The birds that had been singing quite raucously grew still, and soon the only sound was the rattle of the cart's wheels over the hard-packed dirt road. Alizon drew her legs up underneath her. Although the sky overhead was still blue, her limbs felt heavy with cold, and her nose was starting to run. She rubbed at it, then put her hands inside the cap. Her stomach was roiling now, and the very tips of her fingers were prickling. *It's coming*, she thought. *But is it fast enough?*

"What is that? Do you hear it?" John Bowman gestured to Thomas Whittle, who yanked on the reins. The horses stopped. Silence settled over them like a shroud.

"I don't hear nothing," said Whittle, and Alizon had to agree. In the back of the cart, she frowned.

"Shouting. In the woods. What do you mean, you can't hear it?" Bowman stood up in his seat, staring off to their left. He sounded angry already, the tone of a man who is afraid he is being made a fool of. "Don't you lie to me now, Thomas Whittle."

Thomas Whittle seemed at a loss. Alizon turned to look at the wall of trees that John Bowman was so fixated with. No movement there, and no noise.

"What are they shouting?" she asked. John Bowman turned and glared at her, and to her surprise she saw that his cheeks were a hectic red.

"You're jesting with me," he said. His eyes were wet. "I don't know why you'd think this is funny, girl, but mark my words—"

At that moment, the entire cart rocked to one side, as though it had been heavily struck by something from the right-hand side of the woods. John Bowman fell from the cart with a shout, and Alizon found herself thrown into the wall of the cage, pieces of straw showering all over her. The two horses up the front screamed, and again the cart was struck. This time it skewed awkwardly across the road. There was a bellow from Thomas Whittle and then the cart righted itself, only to lurch forward before abruptly stopping again.

'What . . . what happened?'

Alizon got to her feet. There was no one on the driving board of the cart, and both the horses had vanished. She turned in time to see the broad back of Thomas Whittle disappearing into the woods on the far side, running as though all the devils in hell were on his heels.

"Wait! *Wait!*"

Then Alizon looked down. John Bowman lay on the ground, his head towards the trees and his chin tipped up, as though baring his fat white neck to her. One of his arms was red to the elbow, and his stomach had been split lengthways. Thick yellowish ropes had escaped from his gut and were strewn across the hard dirt floor. A second later, and the stench of it hit Alizon. It was a smell of shit and panic, of the butcher's yard and the sick room.

"W-what?"

Alizon backed away from the sight, one hand pressed hard to her mouth. She had seen nothing attack the cart, had heard nothing. John Bowman looked as though he'd been torn apart by some monstrous animal, but there was nothing in the road, no sound of some wolf or bear crashing through the trees. What had happened to him? Was it possible to fall so badly that you burst, like a peach left too long on the tree? Was John Bowman afflicted with some form of corpulent rot? Where had the horses gone?

The birds were singing again. Alizon went to the back of the cart where the door to the cage was situated, hoping that perhaps the blow had broken the lock, but it was still shut fast. She closed both hands around the iron struts and gave it a firm rattle. Nothing. She rattled it again, this time in a different direction. Still nothing. She let go. The rough iron had left red marks on her palms.

"I am alone." The thought summoned up a fresh wave of panic, but she forced herself to take a deep breath, ignoring the stench of John Bowman's bowels. "I am *alone*. So think. If I could get out of here, out of this cage..." If she got out, she would hide in the trees and follow the road to Dyersbrook, skirt around it, and wait until it got dark. When she had cover, she could steal a few things, just enough to keep her going across the wild country—a pair of leather shoes perhaps, fruit, dried meat. She would keep herself hidden as much as possible. And then just...keep going. Leave behind the village, leave behind the killing road. If she could get out.

If she could get out of the cage.

The killing road was not usually busy, but people did travel between the two neighbouring villages, and today it would likely see more than usual; few things pried men and women from their chores and daily lives like a burning. They expected to kill her at midday, and who would want to miss that? There would be people at Demdike Hill already—the men John Bowman had paid to build the pyre, the men with ropes and kindling, the men with sticks to make certain the flames leapt higher. They would eventually wonder what had happened to the cart. They would come looking. Eventually.

Ignoring the stinking corpse on the ground, Alizon began to walk slowly around the cart, forcing herself to consider each part of it. She ran her hands over the places where the iron had been riveted to the wood; she got down on her knees and examined each board for weaknesses, curled her nails under every edge. She paid particular attention to the side where the cart had apparently been struck, hoping to find some damage there, but there was nothing. Finally, she stood and pushed against the iron struts, thinking that perhaps part of it might have come loose. It did not move at all.

SEVEN DEAD SISTERS

Alizon had just decided to try the door of the cage a second time when her stomach cramped viciously, sending her to the floor again. A cold sweat sprung out across her forehead and under her arms. She screwed up her eyes, groaning.

Oh yes, she thought. *I had almost forgotten.*

Chapter Two

When it was clear that the friends and neighbours she had grown up with were going to kill her, Alizon had asked for a visit from Goodie Pipkin. When they spoke of the devil and black dogs and laming horses, they whispered Alizon Grey's name, but anyone with any sense in that place knew that Missus Pipkin was the real wise woman—the difference was, Goodie was the one they went to for help. Goodie had nursed fevers, delivered babies, even banished the pox. She was too valuable to burn.

When she came, she wore a hood and wrapped her frail old woman's body in skeins of wool and cotton, and she peered out at Alizon with eyes as bright as a jackdaw's.

"Quite the spot you're in, Alizon Grey."

At this time, Alizon was being held in John Bowman's barn. There was a pitcher of water—bits of straw floating in it—and a half-eaten bowl of porridge on the floor. Alizon herself was keeping to the darkest corner, but she scrambled out into the light for Goodie.

"Do you think I had a choice?"

Goodie Pipkin turned her face away. "I can't do nothing for you, girl. Your redemption now lays on Demdike Hill, God save you.

SEVEN DEAD SISTERS

Although why He'd do that, I don't rightly know. Why'd you ask for me, anyway? We two ain't blood. Far from it."

"Who else should I ask to see? Joanie?" For a strange moment, Alizon thought she would laugh. She pulled her fingers down over her lips, chasing the unwanted mirth away. "I won't ask you to save me, Missus Pipkin, but I do ask for your mercy. Have you ever been to a burning?"

The old woman pursed her lips.

"I have," Alizon continued. "My father was right keen on taking us, if you remember. Said it would remind us to live good lives, for the flames at the pyre were nothing to the flames of hell. They burned a man for heresy up on Demdike hill when I was nine years old, and it took him an hour to die, all in all, though from the sounds he was making at the end I do not think he was a man so much as he was a desperate beast. His hair burnt up like a halo around his head. His eyes dripped like candles…"

"What do you *want*, Alizon Grey?" snapped Goodie. A hand had crept out of her woollen wraps and the white fingers were curled around the simple wooden cross at her throat. "Drip your last drops of poison elsewhere."

"I'm sorry. It's something that's playing on my mind a little." Alizon looked down at her hands. "I don't want to die that way, Missus Pipkin."

A silence pooled between them for a short time. Within it, Alizon could hear the shuffling footsteps and sighs of the man guarding the barn door. His name was Henry Smith, and when his wife had been sick, she and her younger sister Joan had picked apples for him. Now he waited with a cudgel in case she should try to see the outside world again.

"What do you expect me to do about it?" Goodie said eventually.

"You would make me say the words?"

Goodie sighed, and after a glance at the barn door, took a step forward. From within the folds of her woollens she pulled out a small linen bag, which she passed to Alizon. Inside it was a folded leaf, and on the inside of that had been smeared a thick, brown paste. It smelled sharp, but not necessarily unpleasant.

"Eat the whole thing," she said briskly. "Be warned, it'll not take you straight away, girl, so do what you will in plenty of time. Do not try and eat it just before they cast you on the flames."

"Thank you." Alizon looked at the leaf a moment longer, then put it back in the small bag and hid it under the straw. "You are a good woman."

Goodie looked displeased at that. "Am I now? You know well that to take your own life is to send yourself to hell just as quickly. And I am helping you to do that."

"If there is a hell, Missus Pipkin, I imagine the chances of me escaping it are slim."

The old woman nodded, and the portion of face Alizon could see beneath the hood grew sterner. "Mind me, then, girl. Don't leave it too late."

She almost had, though. When Goodie Pipkin had left—stepping into the daylight and flitting away like a crow—Alizon had looked at the poison again. She hadn't asked the wise woman what it was, or how it worked, but she had little doubt it would do what it was supposed to. With the means of her own death in her hands, a death that would not crisp her skin or blacken her bones, she found herself reluctant, still.

I'll wait as long as I can, she had thought. *You never know. The village could be stricken with plague. A storm could blow the barn roof off. The hand of God Himself could reach down from the sky and pluck me to safety.*

So she waited. And waited. And when she heard them coming to the door, the men who would take her to Demdike Hill, only then had she eaten the leaf and its paste, chewing it quickly and washing it down with tepid water from the pitcher. It had tasted of bile and dark roots, and her heart had seemed to float up through her chest.

There's no more time.

Chapter Three

I **CAN'T GET OUT. BUT WHAT IF I COULD? WHAT IF** there is a chance I don't have to die today?
Alizon got down on her knees in the furthest corner of the cart and bent over. She hooked two fingers into her mouth and poked, and her guts clenched like a fist. A surge of bile came up her throat and she retched it into the straw, again and again until it felt like she might be empty. The sick that came up looked clear and innocuous, no sign of the leaf or its paste. She had eaten nothing else that morning. *Perhaps it's already in me, Goodie's poison. Perhaps it's too late.*

She spat into the straw and wiped her mouth. Her stomach still hurt, although now she wasn't sure if that was simply from vomiting. After a moment, she kicked some of the straw over the mess she had left and turned her eye to the world outside the cart. If she met someone alone on the road, there was a chance she could convince them to let her out. There was some sort of beast in the woods. Surely no one would choose to leave her to be torn apart?

On the road though, no one came. Alizon paced back and forth in the cage, looking first up the road, trying to spot where the horses might have gone, and then back down it, trying to guess who would be the first to come up towards Demdike Hill. The morning was getting properly underway; the first chills of dawn had withdrawn into the trees, and the sky overhead was a more confident blue. There were wisps of cloud edging over from the east, but it was a largely windless day. No one came. The horses didn't return. Of Thomas Whittle, there was no sign.

Which left only John Bowman.

One hand pressed to her pained stomach, she peered reluctantly down at his corpse, and for a moment was startled enough that she felt a wave of pins move through her entire body. He had moved. Just a little—the arm that had looked like it was digging in his own guts lay clear in the dirt now. She could see the dark circles under his fingernails.

"You didn't look properly before, Alizon, that's all," she said aloud. "And who can blame you? Look well now—no man can survive his lights all spread at his feet. He's dead."

A fly was already crawling on the pale flesh of his neck. Another had alighted on a thick rope of his innards, tasting his blood in that delicate way flies have.

When she had been around seven or eight, she and her sister Meredith had started to see a skinny mongrel dog on the outskirts of the village. It was a stray; its ribs stuck through its thin wormy skin, and its ears were ragged flaps. They would see it at the very edge of their yard, slinking back into the long grass, or they'd see it trotting across the village square, its nose pointing at the floor. She and Meredith got to be fond of it, like the dog was another villager they would see out and about, someone to wave to and wish a good morning. Their father though, and the other men of the village, would drive the animal off with sticks, or throw stones at it. When Meredith asked why, their father would say that a hungry dog with no master was a dangerous thing, that it had been sniffing around the chicken coops, easing itself closer to the baby goats. And one day the

SEVEN DEAD SISTERS

dog did get its dinner; Missus Riley's chickens were bitten up and torn apart, feathers scattered everywhere and dotted with scarlet drops.

There you are, said their father. Do you see?

Alizon still felt sorry for the dog. When she saw it creeping around their grass again she went to it, intending to shoo it away—she knew what her father would do if he saw the animal. But when she held out her hand to it the dog leapt forward and sank its teeth into her hand, piercing the fat pad of her thumb and sending a hot jolt of agony up her arm. She screamed, but when her father came he looked hard at her, his bristly face split into a grin.

"You see girl," he had said. "The mutt has a taste for it now. It enjoyed the squawk of chickens and it came back for the squawks of a girl. Got a taste for blood, he has."

And you should know, thought Alizon.

That autumn, their father had started to turn on Meredith like an angry dog himself. She was a year older than Alizon, a doughty girl with a stubborn set to her face and a slight curl to her hair, and if anyone teased her sisters Meredith would find them and thump them, pleased to be dispensing justice. They all saw it, even Mother; the way Father watched her movements, his face suddenly dark.

Alizon went into the woods at night, secretly, and she found five silver birch trees growing together in a knot. In the snug little space they made between them, she began to leave tiny treasures—an acorn, an old coin, a piece of wool dyed purple. She added to it every night for a fortnight, asking for a shield for Meredith, for their father's eye to pass over her.

Birch trees, she whispered to the roots, *carry my message to your queen. Don't let him take Meredith, our protector.*

But one autumn evening, when the days were shrinking into themselves like bacon left on a hot stove, Meredith went walking in the woods and never came back.

"That girl," their father said to them, as they sat obedient around the fire. "She always did have a roving eye. We couldn't have kept her here if we tried. Born wilful, she was." He grinned his hard grin at them all, looking fat and satisfied. Their mother kept her head low, her eyes on the stew pot. Occasionally she would stir it, letting fat chunks of pale meat roll to the surface and disappear again.

Alizon went back to the birch trees and dug out all her treasures, threw them into the undergrowth and angrily wiped her cheeks dry.

Chapter Four

In the cart, Alizon stared at the body of John Bowman until her stomach started to roil again. The question of what had killed him—what had hit the cart and sent Thomas Whittle running into the woods—was like a blind spot. Like looking at the sun, she couldn't consider it for very long.

It was getting hotter. The sun was almost directly overhead now, and the road was wide enough that the shade didn't reach her. Restlessly she moved around the back of the cart, but there was no shade anywhere aside from the thin bars afforded by the struts of her cage. Her throat, so recently coated with bile, was dry and uncomfortable, catching every time she swallowed. The last drink she'd had was that quick gulp of tepid water in Bowman's barn; it seemed impossible that she hadn't thought to drink more of it. Suddenly, the idea of cold water was irresistible. *I thought that was my last drink. Why didn't I make more of it?*

Eventually she sat in the corner that was the furthest from the stinking corpse, her head bowed over her knees.

Just rest. Someone will come. Stop looking for them, and they will come.

She was unsure how much time passed. The sun sat heavy on the back of her neck, and when she came back to herself her nostrils were filled with the smell of burning. Panic turned a sickly loop in her chest, but when she jumped to her feet she was still in the back of the cart—not tied to the pyre, watching the edges of her skirts catch. Instead, she saw a thick plume of black smoke hanging over the trees, back down the road. Towards the village.

"That's not right."

None of it was right. What could be burning so fiercely in the village to cause that much smoke? It looked like the smoke from a pyre, but Demdike Hill was the other way. Had the cart been turned around more than she thought when it was struck? Was she facing the wrong way now?

But why would they burn the pyre if she wasn't there?

Without really knowing why, Alizon pressed her face between the iron bars at the back of the cart and shouted.

"Help! I'm stuck here! Where are you all?"

The words set out bravely down the road then seemed to drop, like stones. The silence left in their wake was stark. Alizon pressed her hand to her lips. It had been a mistake to make any noise—whatever had killed John Bowman would hear her and come back. She stood, one hand gripping an iron strut so tightly her knuckles turned white, but nothing, and no one, came for her. She sat back down again.

Chapter Five

Alizon's sister Anne was a year younger than her, and they grew up together as close as the egg white and the yolk; when she thought of her childhood, Alizon thought first of Anne's small hand in her fist. Anne was slight and had yellow hair like their mother, and slightly protuberant eyes, so that some of the boys in the village used to call her Minnow, a name she did not completely dislike. Together they were aware of the danger that was their father in the way that cows know when a thunderstorm is coming, and the year that Alizon turned twelve and Anne turned eleven, that storm was constantly on the edge of hearing. They went into the woods together and, after cutting their palms with a piece of jagged flint, they smeared their blood onto a likely looking rock and asked the faeries for protection, again. Alizon was sure, if they could just do it the right way, they could ally the hidden folk to their cause. Didn't they seek out the wicked? And blood, she was almost sure of it, had to be the right gift. Milk hadn't worked. Treasure hadn't worked.

The two sisters left their blood on the stone in autumn, and the winter that followed on after was a howling, bitter thing. Snow fell four feet deep, and their family was trapped inside their small house.

Only Father was tall and strong enough to go outside, and he went out often, bringing back firewood, beer, food scrounged from other households. Ice crept in at the edges of the floorboards, and they all huddled around the smoky fire, their hands chaffed and bluish. Days were lost in a white thunder of silence, and they all spoke less and less. Father seemed to grow weary of seeing them by the fire, and soon he was curling his lip every time he stepped in the door.

"Have you women nothing else to do?" he said. "I am sick of the sight of ye. You look like miserable, starveling babes."

The weather grew worse as they entered the very howling heart of winter. The people of the village barely had enough to eat themselves, let alone share, and they went through the last of their preserves and dried, salted meat. The goats, who had been brought indoors, stopped giving milk, and it seemed to Alizon that her father began to watch them all even more closely. Once, when she had reached for a piece of wood to put on the fire, he had reached out and grabbed her arm, squeezing it hard enough to rub her bones together. He let her go, but she saw him do the same to Anne, almost lifting her up off the rug. Anne squealed like a pig, and for reasons Alizon couldn't name a black terror moved through her, making the hair on the back of her neck stand up. She remembered what her father had said about the dog.

Got a taste for it.

A few nights later, Alizon woke to hear the wind moaning around the house, making the boards creak and the chimney scream. The remains of the fire in the hearth flickered uncertainly; they were all of them packed around it, sleeping so close they were frequently scorched. But she'd been woken by the sound of footsteps, and as she lifted her head, she saw her father with Anne. His thick fist was clasped around her tiny, bony shoulder, and he was guiding her into the other room. Alizon half-rose from where she was, every sense pricking awake, but her mother leaned down from her chair and held her where she was. Their mother was a quiet woman, and she did all she could to avoid looking into the eyes of her children, but that night she looked directly at Alizon—her face was made from pieces of shadow and red firelight. It looked like a face from hell.

"Don't," she said.

Not long after that, winter lost its bite, and spring's green fingers thawed away the snow and ice. Anne wasn't mentioned again. Lots of villagers lost family members during that cold time, the very young and the greatly aged, and to dwell on it was seen to be unlucky. The spring had come eventually, hadn't it? What more did you want? Cursing the winter was the quickest way to bring it back.

When the earth had warmed through and the dirt was soft again, Alizon went out under the cover of darkness and made her way to the spot where the unnamed baby had been buried. She knew it like she knew the freckle on the back of her wrist. There, she dug down with pick and hands until she reached a rotten roll of ragged cloth, and in the light of the full moon she could see that it was stiff with old bloodstains—christening shawl and winding shroud, all at once, it seemed. There was nothing else of the child, no mouldering flesh and no bones. No bones at all.

Chapter Six

THE DAY WAS GROWING HOTTER. ALIZON LAY ON her back in the cart, looking up through the iron cage at the sky. Her lips felt dry and cracked already; every now and then she would run the tip of her finger across them. Still, no one from the village came, and no one from Demdike Hill, which made no sense to her at all. Judging by the sun in the sky, her time of burning had come and gone, yet those godly men on the hill, with their sticks and ropes, hadn't come down the road for them. They would have horses themselves, she reasoned, or some of them would, but as quietly as she lay and as hard as she listened, there came no sound of hoofbeats on the beaten dirt, no footsteps, no voices calling out. With the warmth and the silence, Alizon began to doze. After a while it seemed to her that she wasn't in a cage—she was at home, in their scratchy piece of garden, and it was the middle of summer, hot enough that the air seemed to hum. All of the plants were growing green and lush, so full of life she felt like she could almost see their thin limbs reaching up to the light, and her sisters were there, all of them, together, which she knew made no sense. Mother was an indistinct shape at the edge of the ground, bent over to pull some root from the black dirt, and Father wasn't there at all.

SEVEN DEAD SISTERS

"You're all here." It was hard to focus, but that in itself was pleasant. She felt like she'd drunk a lot of small beer on an empty stomach. "Even the baby."

The girls turned and looked at her, smiling. Meredith looked older, more careworn somehow, and Alizon thought: *she learnt something important in the woods, and it changed her*. Anne, her little minnow, was sitting with a baby in her lap, a fat healthy baby almost as big as her.

Jenny, her oldest sister was there, and her face was a little blurred, as though it had been held underwater. Alizon had last seen Jenny when she was two or three years old.

"Alizon," said Jenny. Her voice was warm. "What have you done to your hands?"

She looked down. Her hands were curled against her apron, and they were black and red raw, the skin charred and smoking. The bones peeked out through her knuckles, glistening in the heat of the fire.

"NO!"

Alizon woke up in the cart, scrambling up and crashing into the bars. For a second, when she looked at her hands *they were still burned*... and then the illusion was gone. She fell to her knees, her stomach seized with cramps and her head thumping.

"They didn't burn me," she insisted to the boards of the cart, but she was afraid to look at her hands. She snatched up her white cloth cap and hid her hands inside it. "They didn't bloody burn me yet."

The shadows had changed, and when she looked up she saw that the sky had lost its midday brightness. There was still a pall of smoke hanging over the trees, and the edges of the road were clothed in a deeper darkness. The clouds had started to come in—she had slept through most of the day into dusk, and the idea frightened her quite badly. The beast that had killed John Bowman and chased off Thomas Whittle could have come back, could have padded its way around the cart, looking at her sleeping body. She could have woken to the cage being shaken apart.

The road was still empty.

"Hello? Hello!" Her fear of the beast couldn't quite keep her from calling out. The silence, the smoke, the absence of anyone coming to see what had happened to the condemned woman, the absence of anyone at all on the road—all of it was scratching at her nerves. Perhaps there had been some great cataclysm. Meredith had told her once of an entire town that had fallen deep into the earth—every man, woman and child swallowed up in a handful of seconds. Alizon hadn't believed it at the time, but what did she know about anything, really? It could be that these things happened all the time. "Is anyone still alive out there?"

"I would say not, personally."

She froze. The voice had come wheedling up from the ground beyond the cart. Only one thing lay there. A thing that should not be able to talk.

Reluctantly, she sidled over to the edge of the cart. The corpse of John Bowman lay where she'd last seen it. Already it looked like it was swelling up. His skin had turned tight and yellow.

"This is the killing road, or that's what they call it," said John Bowman. As he spoke his head shifted slightly, pulling his chin down into his neck. Eyes that looked as dry and wrinkled as old peas turned slowly to look at her. "Certainly feels like it to me."

"What...what are you?"

"I don't rightly know, girl. Where is Thomas Whittle? Why is he not with the cart?"

"He ran off into the woods." Alizon bit her lip. There seemed to be a cold wind rushing through her head. "Something frightened him. Did you see...did you see what did it? What came out of the trees?"

The head rolled a little away from her. His lips, which were a livid purple colour, smacked together briefly.

"It was big. The biggest living thing I have seen. It thundered down, its shadow cold. There were horns, antlers, things alive in the spaces between them."

"That's nonsense," said Alizon. Her eyes moved down John Bowman's body to focus on his festering guts. The flies there were quite lively now. "Things like that don't live in these woods. They don't live in any woods."

"Perhaps beasts like that have always been here. Perhaps they've been here longer than we have, did you ever think of that, Alizon Grey? Who can say what was here before we were? Before men and women crept out of that first garden, shamed and feeling the cold for the first time on their naked hides. Perhaps they've always been here, and we're just seeing them now, on the killing road."

Alizon took a half-step backwards. The white cap had dropped from her fingers; they felt numb, like they belonged to someone else.

"You don't sound like old John Bowman. And what do you know about anything? You're dead."

John Bowman laughed, a rusty whistle of a noise. "I can see a great many things you can't, girl."

"I need to get out of here. Out of this cage. Before whatever that thing was comes back. Do you have the key?"

"Of course I do. It's right in my pocket here."

"Give it to me."

The corpse laughed all the harder at that. "Even if I could, I wouldn't."

"You can move," pointed out Alizon. "Your lips are moving now. You moved your head."

"I'm all broken inside, girl. I might be twitching at you, but my days of turning keys in locks, or dancing a jig, or wringing your neck... well, they are gone far from me now, more's the pity."

"You pig."

Alizon got down on the floor of the cart and stuck her arm out through the gap in the struts. She reached as far as she could, pressing the side of her face into the dirty straw and stretching her arm so far she felt her shoulder twang with the effort of it, but even at her furthest reach John Bowman's boot was still a good foot away. Swearing oaths under her breath, she stood up and brushed herself off.

"Does it hurt?" she asked eventually.

There was a period of silence before the corpse answered. His blood, she saw, had largely sunk into the dirt road, the long hours of sun turning it dark and sticky.

"I'm surprised such things concern you, Alizon Grey. The pains you put your father through…"

"Him!" A familiar tightness bloomed behind Alizon's breastbone. She no longer knew if it was guilt or fury. "You people. No interest in our little family while me and my sisters were suffering. Oh, I saw the occasional raised eyebrow when I went to the well, and I've no doubt you dragged out our business amongst you when you were in your cups, but did any of you raise a hand to help? Or did all the Grey girls seem alike to you?"

John Bowman said nothing.

"You hold yourself to be a man of the law, Master Bowman, so where was the law when my sisters were dying?"

"A man's family and how he disciplines them is no concern of the law."

Alizon gave a surprised bark of laughter. She turned away from him, then turned back, clasping her hands around the bars. "Discipline? Is that what you supposed it to be? You wouldn't discipline a dog the way my father did us. Or you'd end up with a lot of dead dogs. My God, you people." All around them the last light was seeping out of the day, and the air was growing cool again. Alizon remembered her hand closing around the wooden handle of the mallet, how the weight of it had been comforting. "You call yourselves godly, but none of you lifted a finger. Happy to turn the other cheek though, oh yes."

"Do you imagine you'll go to heaven when you burn, Alizon Grey?"

Alizon squeezed the iron bars. Hell was a small house in the grip of an endless winter, where words stop and something that shares your blood watches you too closely. Hell is the space where a baby's bones should be.

"I don't fear what happens to me after I die," said Alizon. "Although, if I had your fate…"

The corpse of John Bowman had stopped moving. The idea of prompting him to speak felt too much like admitting she needed the company. Alizon walked to the far end of the cart again, and sat down, looking out at the road that led back to the village.

Chapter Seven

After Meredith went into the woods and didn't come back, Alizon took to walking there alone, whenever she could get time away from chores and helping her mother. She sang in the woods, and tried to make herself receptive to the fair folk that might be sleeping on the mosses or hiding in the brambles. The stories she'd heard suggested that they liked to spirit away children who sang well, or who were exceptionally beautiful. She brushed her hair and washed her face before she went there. She looked for escape into a realm that never saw the night, or winter.

"Where are you? I've offered you everything. Where is your protection?"

Although she would periodically stop and listen, holding her breath and wishing very hard, she never heard the faint silvery tinkle of faery bells, or the laughter of beings that would prove to be beautiful yet cruel. The woods seemed to be empty of faeries, and empty of Meredith.

The sun had set. Alizon stood up, blinking warily. She felt like she'd been in the cart for a hundred years; she felt like she'd only just stepped up into it, the hissing and glaring of her neighbours falling on the back of her neck like frigid January rain. Time felt...wrong.

Panic surged up in her chest then, closing a cold hand around her throat. She took hold of the cage door and shook it with all the strength she had, muscles standing out like cords in her arms and neck. She threw herself against the door, twice, then again circled the cart, looking for weaknesses. At some point she realised she was sobbing, her chest hitching and stuttering as tears oozed down her dirty cheeks. Nothing about this made any sense. Where were the people from Demdike Hill? What had happened at the village? Hunger and thirst were a real problem now, and her head felt thundery and light, like a pebble rolled inside a milk churn. With the sun vanished beyond the tree tops, darkness had seeped across the road from the trees and slowly eaten up every inch of the cart. Alizon looked down at her hands, which were now little more than familiar shapes in the gloom.

"It'll get darker yet," said John Bowman. Reluctantly Alizon shuffled over to his side of the cart. He looked like a stain on the ground. "You'll see. Or you won't, I suppose."

"Where is everyone?"

The corpse of John Bowman rolled his head to one side, away from her.

"Where are *you*, Alizon Grey?"

Alizon placed her hands flat against the bars again, concentrating on the feel of them, the rough cold solidity. With the darkness growing deeper all around, the idea that she was already dead was starting to feel alarmingly possible. The poison that Goodie had given her had already carried her off perhaps, twitching and foaming on the floor of the cart, or she had already made her journey up to Demdike Hill, and all that was left of her was some smoking bones and a few hot pools of congealing fat.

If she was dead, though, what was this place?

"I had a sister called Mary. You must remember her. She was the only one of us with black hair, like our father." Alizon crouched down, putting her back to the darkness of the woods and resting her eyes on the gloomy shape of John Bowman. "Do you remember her?"

When Bowman said nothing, she continued.

"I will tell you this—I did not like Mary much. She was six years younger than me, born the year after Mother…lost another baby. That black hair wasn't the only sign of our father's blood in her. She had a hard heart. I never saw her cry, not once, and us Grey children had lots of reasons to cry. Once, in the late summer, Anne had spent all day gathering blackberries. I caught Mary carrying them outside, her little fists purple with juice. She wasn't eating them, just mushing them between her fingers and dropping the ruined mess into the dirt. Her little face was so intent. She was…three or four years old?'

"You think that is evil, in the face of what you did?" John Bowman muttered.

"No, you don't understand. She liked to break things for the sake of it. And I thought, at least that will keep her safe from him. You see? She must be his favourite, I thought." Alizon lifted her eyes from the corpse of John Bowman and looked into the trees. They were a single dark mass now. The wind was a rustling presence. "Do you remember her at all, John Bowman?"

"Small girls…all look the same to me."

"Really? You remembered my face readily enough, when it was time to lock me in that barn." Alizon rubbed a hand over her face. It was starting to get very cold. "Are you sure you don't remember Mary? When she was seven, when she had a year left in this world still, she killed a neighbour's kitten. It caused much upset. And being such a concerned man, John Bowman, so concerned over his neighbour's moral failings, I would have thought you would remember that."

"Harry Liefsson," he said quietly, surprising Alizon. "His cat was

SEVEN DEAD SISTERS

the best mouser in the village, and he thought to make a few pennies selling off those kittens. But a little girl got hold of one of them."

"That's right," Alizon said. She shuffled forward slightly on her knees, lowering her voice. Speaking loudly in this dark felt like taunting the devil. "She said she wanted to play with them, and she was a sweet looking thing really, Mary, big eyes, big blue eyes like a painted doll. None of them thought she would hurt anything, but I could have told them. But none of you ever listened to me, did you? I did what I could to protect Anne, my little minnow, but Mary. I thought she would live a charmed life. That's what I thought."

"How did she…"

"How did she die? Is that what you mean to ask, John Bowman?"

The corpse said nothing.

"It was a bad summer. The heat turned all the grass yellow, do you remember? Old graves in the churchyard began to show themselves again as the earth shrank into itself, and I thought to myself at the time, well, that can hardly be a good omen, can it? But then we never did have good ones. Only bad ones." Alizon shivered all over. In the midst of the cold dark the heat of that distant summer felt impossible. She struggled to remember how it felt to have the sun heavy on your head; to feel your skin prickling to a dark pink across your shoulders. "Crops failed, our gardens withered. Things stopped growing and died in the earth."

"You are babbling, child."

Alizon shook herself. "We were *hungry* again. Mary was eight years old by then, and a proper little madam. She wouldn't take instruction from me, or any of us, and she would even roll her eyes at our father when she felt like it. She didn't really know, I don't think, couldn't have known, so why would she have been afraid of him…"

A cold wind blew down the road and Alizon shrank against the bars.

"I *do* remember this child," said John Bowman suddenly. "It was an accident. An unfortunate thing, but hardly something you could lay at your father's door."

"An accident?" Alizon rubbed a hand under her nose; it was beginning to drip with moisture. "To begin with, yes. I…"

She had been there, that day, in the tiny corner of their home that served as a kitchen. Mother had been chopping up the remains of a skinny rabbit with the biggest, sharpest knife they had—it was old and huge, and their father kept it sharp—and Alizon had been soaking some hard beans to make them soft again. Mary had been fussing around them both—she had kept trying to put her hand in the bowl of water Alizon was using for the beans, until Alizon had snapped at the younger girl to get out of her hair. Mary had gone to lean against their mother's legs, and Alizon had looked away. Whatever had happened, had happened in that moment.

"She screamed, and I looked up. The knife had fallen." In the dark, Alizon stopped. Fallen? Dropped? Thrown? "It had fallen and cut Mary, badly."

The heavy blade had torn a ragged path down the girl's thigh, and blood had blossomed dark and heavy on the girl's scruffy little shift. Alizon's confused mind had briefly tried to explain it away—*it's just her bleeding time, that's all, it came so early*—and then their mother had started screaming.

"These things happen," said Bowman, a hint of smugness in his voice. "Ours is a hard life, girl, there are dangers everywhere."

Alizon stood up and wrapped her hands around the bars again. The dark of the night felt thick and alive, like something foul pressed up against her face. "Father took Mary into their room, said she needed rest. They would bind the cut. And I was furious, because none of us had ever been taken there when we were ill, and I thought that proved it, that proved that Mary was the favourite because she had his eyes and his hair." Alizon pressed the back of her hand to her mouth, to suppress a noise somewhere between mirth and horror. "I didn't see her for a week, and then one day I snuck into the room while Father was chopping wood, and I saw Mary in the bed. She had shrunk. Her little face was the colour of milk, and the skin around her eyes was grey. She looked like a pale little mushroom, sprouting in the dark, and I felt bad for her—the only time I ever did, I suppose. I sat on the bed and patted her leg and…it wasn't there."

"What do you mean?" snapped Bowman.

"Just a little stump. I pulled back the blanket and…Bound tightly with scraps, but red and oozing all the same." Alizon leaned her head against the bars, closed her eyes. Of all the horrors, why was this one so hard to think on? "I asked my mother *why*, and she told me the knife had been dirty. It had turned the wound bad, and the only way…"

"A fever from a cut, yes," said Bowman, a little primly. "That is what we were told."

"Mary died the next day. *We were told*. I didn't see what they buried." She took a long, shaky breath. "Do you not see that my father was the devil? Surely you can see that now, John Bowman? He was the *devil*."

He said nothing. Alizon stepped away from the bars and walked to the far side of the cart. She felt cold down to her very bones, and the tingling in the tips of her fingers had turned into an alarming kind of blankness. Beyond the cart there was silence. She opened her mouth to speak again, although she didn't know what she was going to say, and something huge rushed out of the darkness ahead of her. A second or so beforehand she would have sworn it was too dark to see anything clearly, but then the dark itself seemed to be given form. Alizon threw herself backwards in a panic and then the thing hit the cart, raising it off its wheels and Alizon off her feet.

When she crashed down against the bare wooden boards, the corpse of John Bowman was screaming; a terrible high-pitched noise, like a pig being slaughtered. Alizon pressed herself flat to the floor, the stench of old wood and urine in her nostrils. Her mind had been blasted blank by the noise, by the sudden violence, by the proximity of the creature. She could *feel* the heat of it, warmth blasting off it like a hot stove.

Look at it, she told herself, one lone thought rattling around in her head. *Look at it, face what it is.*

But she couldn't.

Bowman had stopped screaming. The cart rocked again, back and forth and then *over*, and Alizon screamed herself as she was thrown onto the bars, the freezing metal crashing into her back.

And then silence again.

For the longest time, Alizon did not move. Despite the pain in her back and the fear closing her throat, she lay where she had fallen awkwardly against the bars with her eyes tightly shut. She held her breath and listened—no sounds from the corpse, no wind in the trees, and no movement at all from the creature. Was it sitting still now, inches away, watching her with baleful eyes? Wanting her to move, the way cats want mice to move?

I can't hear its breath, she told herself firmly. *It's gone.*

She opened her eyes. The world had taken on a strange angle. Gradually she realised that the creature had managed to tip the cart over onto its side, and it had landed on the body of John Bowman, sending everything askew. On the heels of that thought was the realisation that it wasn't so dark anymore—the creature had chased some of the dark out, and the moon rushed behind tattered clouds.

She sat up. The places where the bars had struck her were throbbing. She looked to her left and saw the shape that was John Bowman. In the cold moonlight she could see his guts, glistening faintly and oozing around the iron struts. Of his face she could see nothing; his body ended at the neck now, ragged tatters of flesh lying on the killing road.

"That's it for you," she whispered. "No more talk from you, John

Bowman. I didn't hope to see your death today but perhaps God grants us small pleasures after all."

Alizon edged towards him and reached through the bars to his trouser pocket. Her hand brushed the broken loop of his insides, and for a second it seemed to cling horribly, like skin on a pudding, but then her hands closed around the iron key and she yanked it out. Carefully, she climbed to the rear end of the cart and slotted the key into the lock there. The door fell open with a crash and she slipped out of it as fast as a fish flitting from a bucket.

Chapter Eight

O UT ON THE ROAD, ALIZON STOPPED, HALF-CROUCHING like a rabbit that had taken fright. She stayed like that for some time, the sound of her own breathing whistling in her ears, one question circling her mind.

Where to go where to go

As desperate as she had been to get out of the cage, she now felt exposed, and the road did not feel safe. Where had the beast gone? The cold light of the flickering moon showed her the rutted lines of the dirt path, but she could not see any animal tracks. It had to have vanished into the woods, and yet she was drawn to the treeline anyway.

You can't go in there, she told herself. *That is where the creature went. Where it took old John Bowman's head.*

She went though, her feet making no sound at all on the road, and when she passed across the line of trees into the forest she shivered once, hard, her teeth gritted and her hands clenched into fists. Amongst the trees a new world of sounds opened up; the crackle of her footsteps as they crunched old twigs and dry leaves into new shapes, the shifting hustle of air moving through branches, the soft calls of some night bird as hungry as any winter morning. As she went

SEVEN DEAD SISTERS

she thought of her sisters' names, said them over and over in her head, hissed them through her dried lips, naming her sisters one by one by one. She said their names, and she walked deeper into the woods that crowded to the side of the killing road.

Jenny. Meredith. Anne. Bethan. Mary.
Joan.

Chapter Nine

Joan was born a year or so after Mary, a narrow, pale-faced baby who was unnaturally quiet. Alizon had turned seven that year, and would go and peer into the crib—so recently vacated by Mary—and look down at this strange child, who would be looking back up at her, blue eyes narrowed. As the baby grew, Alizon became convinced that Joan was a changeling, a faery child left in place of the real sister she should have had. She was sure, as Joan became small and slight with a long face, that if she pushed Joan into the fire, she would turn back into the lump of silver birch the faeries had fashioned her from, or whoosh straight up the chimney and into the night, her long limbs dangling.

Meredith, Alizon, Anne, Mary and Joan—they were quite the gang at that time, a gaggle of geese, their father would call them, too noisy for his liking. They were two years away from Meredith vanishing in the woods, five years away from the bitter winter that saw the end of Anne, seven years from Mary's foreshortening. For a while it almost seemed that they might be safe, because there were simply so many of them, so many small girls, hot hands clasped in each other's fists, the baby Joan dandled on Meredith's knee and Mary beginning to toddle, to find things she could break. At first Alizon did not think to ask the faeries for Joan's protection—she was one of their own, after all—and there were good, warm summers, rain in the spring, and some mild winters. Their father still looked at them over his hard grin, but he was busy and often outside, drinking small beer with the neighbours and hunting. There were deer in the woods then, rabbits, pheasant. If you were quick.

Now, in the cold woods by the side of the killing road, Alizon slowly came to a stop. The names in her head faded, and she remembered where she was. She had left the road far behind her somewhere, and in her fear she had walked without thinking. Should she have followed the road back to the village? The idea of seeing a familiar place was attractive, but what would they do? Lock her up again of course, find another day to burn the last Grey girl. In the end, what had happened to John Bowman and Thomas Whittle didn't change what she had done.

She could have walked onwards towards Dyersbrook; stolen what she needed to live and moved on to some unimaginable place beyond. Somehow the thought of walking all that way on the killing road, utterly alone, with the trees on either side watching her…somehow the thought of that would not sit still in her head. So.

"So I don't know where I am, or where I should go," she said aloud. It was getting lighter. The moon had gone, and the trees that loomed on all sides were painted with the silvery lilac light of dawn. "I will walk to keep myself warm, at least."

She did so, trying and failing to walk quietly through the undergrowth, in case the creature was near. Gradually, dawn began to rinse its weak light through the trees and the forest became livelier. Morning birds chattered at each other above her head, the dim hum of insects becoming a background to everything. Slowly, slowly, her shoulders grew slack, and some of the tension she had been holding in her chest eased. With the passing of the dark the world seemed less strange, and more natural concerns began to make themselves known.

She was exhausted and hungry, and her throat felt clogged with sawdust. The weak sunshine did little to warm her through the lattice of branches so despite her steady walk she shivered nearly continually, which in turn was making her back ache.

Eventually Alizon came to a muddy stream, so thin and shallow she almost missed it, and here she crouched down and let the icy cold water run over her fingers. She cupped her palm and sipped from it, wincing as the cold hit her teeth.

As Joan grew up, she grew tall and willowy, her long hair the colour of wet straw. She was a quiet and watchful child who kept close to her sisters if she could, always chasing their shadows and not quite joining in. Despite her initial opinion that Joan was a changeling child, Alizon grew fond of her, and when she placed pebbles in the well for the faeries, she breathed a wish for Joan too—*let her survive us*, she asked, *let my sisters grow big enough to flee this place.*

"You've yet to burn, then."

The voice came from somewhere to her right. Alizon flinched and stood, ready to run deeper into the forest—how strange that the energy to run was suddenly there at her command—and then she saw the broken-down figure at the edge of the stream. A wave of horror moved through her, making the edges of her vision grow dim.

It was Thomas Whittle. Although he was barely recognisable as such. The figure at the edge of the stream had clearly once been a man; she could see his familiar black hair, and his old leather boots caked in black mud. He had been crouching, it looked like, perhaps to scoop some water from the stream just as she had been doing, but then the forest had taken him back.

"What happened to you?"

Handfuls of long, bristling grass burst from rents in his trousers. The flesh on his arms, turning brown and putrid, was pocked with clusters of moss, thick and green and vital, while colonies of mushrooms burst from the corners of his mouth, pushed up through

SEVEN DEAD SISTERS

the thin, stubbled skin on his neck. One of his eyes was gone completely, the hole filled in with inkcap fungus. A small shrub had grown up from the soil and straight through his chest cavity; Alizon could see the buttons of his coat through its narrow branches. It appeared to have pinned him in place.

When he spoke, his voice sounded muffled and strange.

"There's nothing like the burning of a girl. They are beacons in my life, these burnings. The heat from the fire as it catches, the first flicker as it nibbles the hems of their delicate dresses."

"What are you talking about?" Alizon took a step towards him. She no longer felt frightened of him. She didn't know how she felt. "Do you not see what has happened to you?"

"The first time I saw one, I was a boy. My father took me. He said it would do me the power of good to see what happened to those what sinned in God's sight. He told me that women were extra wicked because it is in their nature to lead men to sin, and it was our duty to witness what happened to such. Her name was Elizabeth Smith, and they said she had put the evil eye on a man's flock and caused the animals to sicken and die, all because he had knocked her down in the street. She was a wild woman herself, her hair long and unwashed, falling down to her breasts, and she shouted as they fixed her on the pyre, calling down curses on the shepherd and all the villagers, and all of us what had gathered there to watch her die. One of the men, he struck her on the jaw and she quietened after that."

Alizon stood over him. He didn't seem able to move.

"And then she burned, oh, she burned." Thomas Whittle's body shuddered. Alizon saw the eyelid on his one remaining eye flicker with some strong emotion. "Her dress caught and it was ablaze so fast, and the flames they licked across her skin like kisses, burning her up. I tried to turn away then, because it seemed to me that she was naked and it was wrong to look at her that way, it was sinful, but my father he took a hold of my collar and he held me in place. Watch her, son, he said. Watch how she goes, and learn. I did. I did learn. She screamed as she burned, and then it became a noise like something that has had its neck wrung, and there was the smell too, high and sweet and hot. No other smell like it, Alizon Grey."

Alizon jumped, brought out of a kind of trance by the mention of her name. For a moment there she had been able to smell the smoke herself.

"You are an idiot and a monster, Thomas Whittle," she said. She was wondering if he had anything to eat on him, any food hidden in his pockets, but the thought of touching him made her skin crawl.

He coughed out something that sounded a little like a laugh. "And none of you knew the half of it, either. How my heart sung at those burnings, every one."

"What happened? What was it that hit the cart? You must have seen it. You ran from it fast enough, and left us both there."

"Once, I was riding back towards the north side of Demdike Hill, and I found a girl there. She had run away from her family because they was too hard on her and she couldn't take it no longer, but she hadn't prepared, no she hadn't. No coat, no shoes fit for a long walk. She was lost and cold and miserable as sin."

Alizon crossed her arms over her chest, feeling cold again. Thomas Whittle clearly had no intention of answering her questions, and it was doing her no good to stop and listen, but she still had no idea where she should go.

"What did you do to her?" she asked, although the heavy feeling in her arms told her she already knew.

"I hit her," Thomas Whittle said, from his place crouched by the stream. As Alizon watched, a shining green beetle crept out of his sleeve and across his hand. She lost it in the grass that sprouted there. "She went down then, aye, a little sleep for a good girl, and I tied her up and had a burning of my very own. You often see smoke over Demdike hill, don't you? Aye, you do. She cried a lot, that one. She was afraid, and she begged me to untie her, as if she didn't know it was me who tied her up in the first place. When it was done, I poked through the hot fat that was left and I kept a little with me, in a bag. I always have it with me, a little piece of that day."

All thought of exploring Thomas Whittle's pockets left Alizon then. Instead, she lifted her foot and kicked him, as hard as she could. His chest fell inwards where she struck it, as if he were hollow inside, and when she kicked again there was indeed a hole—a dark and busy space, like the bole in an old tree. Things moved inside it. He coughed and made a gurgling sound.

"They should have burned *you*," she said, and struck him again. Where her fist hit his head, there was a wet, sucking noise, and his face collapsed a little, revealing brown ridged flesh like the gills of a mushroom. A thin line of brown fluid ran from his slack mouth. "*You* were the monster, not me."

"No," he said, even as his body wilted under the weight of her violence. "The monster is still out here in these woods, and it's coming for you, Alizon. Listen, girl. It's going to find you. It knows your smell, see."

Alizon stopped, suddenly disgusted by the broken form in front of her and the hot smell of decay leaking from it. She turned and walked away from Thomas Whittle, her back straight and her hands held out in front of her, until she lost sight of him. She knelt back to the stream and washed her hands quickly, rubbing them until they were red and raw.

Somewhere in the distance, something huge was crashing through the undergrowth. She had to get moving.

Chapter Ten

ALIZON TROTTED FURTHER DOWNSTREAM AND THEN began to move more slowly. The crashing noises had moved into the distance, and she was suddenly very aware of just how hungry and thirsty she was, so she paused to take a few more handfuls of brackish water from the stream. Then, she began to look more carefully at the undergrowth around her.

All children of the village learned to forage from an early age. In leaner years—and there had been so many lean years—a handful of wild garlic or a capful of bilberries could keep the more lethal hunger pangs from the door. It took some time, but eventually she spotted the soft sproutings of the pignut plant. There were some mushrooms too, but they made her think of the growths sprouting from Thomas Whittle's eye socket, so she let them be. The stem of the pignut was very delicate, and you had to be careful or you could snap it, losing your guide to the nut itself. The best way was to use a long thin stick, to wheedle your way down to the hidden morsels, and Alizon was an old hand. After an hour or so, she had a handful of fat little tubers, which she washed as best she could in the stream, and then she sat and ate them, crunching the nutty flesh between her teeth.

It was quiet again, and with a tiny bit of food in her stomach, she

SEVEN DEAD SISTERS

felt an odd kind of calm settle over her, like a heavy blanket that was too much trouble to lift. Her eyes became unfocused. She was thinking of Joan, just a handful of weeks ago. Under the last full moon, Joanie was still alive.

Chapter Eleven

They were the last two survivors. Their mother had become ill over the previous summer and died wheezing in her bed. Joan had made it to twelve years, a fact that always startled Alizon. How had this sickly baby, with her sallow skin and stick limbs, lived and lived while her vital sisters—stocky Meredith, stubborn Mary—had died? It startled her even more to think that she herself was nineteen, a grown woman, when even Jenny, who had vanished out of their lives so long ago, had been only fifteen when she left. Alizon tried to tell herself that Jenny had gotten out, that she had survived and was living in some other village, far from this cursed place; that Jenny was into her third decade by now and likely had several children of her own. But Jenny remained fifteen in Alizon's heart—and she knew that when she had walked out of their home and into the dark night, it wasn't to any kind of happy ending.

More than old enough for marriage now, Alizon had expected their father to sell her off to some farmer's lad. Hadn't he always complained about how many girls were underfoot? Now was his chance to get rid of one, and a new kind of tension sank into her bones the older she got. She would not go. Couldn't go, not while Joanie was here, and she was prepared to tell her father that, but he did not speak of it. One day, in the weeks after Mother died, a neighbour had come by to give them a pail of milk. Henry, his name was, a bluff, hearty man with ruddy cheeks and calloused hands. He had given Alizon an appraising look as he handed her the pail, and then raised his eyebrows at her father.

"Time to get this one out of the house, I expect. Look at her. My Emma is her age and has weaned two babies already, getting fat with her third. Now then, Elias Grey, you know well I have a son who needs to be set on his own right path—"

"Aye, I know your son," rumbled Alizon's father. He was stood with his arms crossed over his barrel chest.

"Well then." Henry beamed at Alizon's father, his ruddy cheeks like apples. "Shall I bring him over? Sooner started, sooner we'll have a few more grandchildren around the place. They can brighten up a sad home, I dare say…"

"Thank you for the milk, Henry," Alizon's father said, and turned away, heading back inside their small home. Alizon stood for a moment, the pail in her hands, and she saw the combination of expressions that passed over their neighbour's face: surprise, embarrassment, anger. He gave her one furious look, as though the whole thing had been her fault, and then stomped his way out of their garden.

"You should go."

The voice was small, hesitant. Joan stepped out from behind the goat's pen. It was a warm day but she was wearing their mother's old knitted shawl over her shoulders, because she always felt the cold.

"Don't talk nonsense."

"You should, though." Joan came over and slipped one cold hand around Alizon's forearm. *Cold as iron*, Alizon thought. "Get out of this house if you can. Even if it means marrying some idiot boy, wouldn't you be better off elsewhere?" She lowered her voice, her chin dipping into her chest as though she were telling a secret. "Safer, elsewhere."

"Joanie." Alizon put the pail of milk down and turned to her sister. "And leave you here, alone, with him?" Even as she said it she felt a shiver of sickness deep inside; she *wanted* to go, more than anything. Why was Joan the only one who had lived? Why was Joan still here? Shame followed the thought like a cloud and its shadow, and she smiled to try and hide it. "I cannot. You know that. We must wait. Wait for…"

They both knew what they had to wait for, but neither wanted to name it. Their father was as hale and hearty as he had ever been; even the lean times had made little difference to him. There was some other force at work in him, some terrible will that would not let him sicken and grow weak, as their mother had done.

"I am safe," said Joan, and to Alizon's wonder, she even thought her sister believed it. "He won't touch me, not now. There is only me, and I can keep out of his way. And Alizon," she squeezed her forearm with long bony fingers. "If you married, there would be somewhere else I could go. Another roof, in the winter. He cannot stop me visiting my sister, can he? I can survive, while you build your own home. I'll be safe."

Joan wasn't safe.

The day had grown warmer and livelier. Alizon left the trickle of the stream behind and headed deeper into the woods, heading vaguely east, towards Dyersbrook—or so she hoped. She felt filthy and tired, her back still aching from where she had struck the bars of the cage, and her throat was scratchy and dry despite the sips of muddy water. She thought of Goodie Pipkin. Had the old woman given her not poison, but some innocent sludge of dried leaves? It seemed likely, given

SEVEN DEAD SISTERS

she was still standing, but it was a cruel act, something she had been certain the old wise woman was not capable of. Alizon pictured herself being dragged out of the cart and tied to the pyre, panic rising in her chest as they tightened her bonds and lit their tapers, and still she was alive. Alive to feel the first tongues of flame as they licked at her feet, alive to feel her dress crisp to her skin and her hair light up like a candle. She would have screamed and wailed and begged for them to kill her, for as long as she could form words, anyway…

In the forest, she stopped. She could smell smoke.

She looked back towards where she thought her own village must be, thinking of the great pall of black smoke that had been there previously, but this deep within the forest she could see nothing. There were noises though; something large was crashing through the undergrowth again, and it was coming towards her.

In a second she was off, flinging herself forward through the trees and bushes with no thought for the branches and thorns that drew bloody sketches down her arms and legs. She ran with great lolloping strides, moving with the energy of sheer panic, and outside of the sound of her own thundering heart she could hear it still; the beast was coming, and it was getting closer.

Run run run, she thought. *You are one animal in a forest full of them, let it take something else.*

And then as she ran, as if she had summoned them, she saw animals crashing through the undergrowth all around her. There were rabbits and rats and foxes, slippery shifting patterns of brown light too fast to track that were probably deer. She saw squirrels scattering ahead of her; even the birds seemed to be fleeing, the canopy over her head suddenly loud and raucous. She kept going, arms up in front of her face to save it from the brambles even as the long grasses whipped at her legs, and soon she found she was gasping for breath, her lungs burning in her chest.

Alizon stumbled to a stop. She could no longer hear the sound of the beast coming up behind her. Instead, the whole forest was filled with an ominous, familiar crackling, and it was hard to breath. Smoke, grey and hazy, hung between tree trunks. A deer disappeared into it and was lost, like a ghost.

"Fire." Alizon coughed violently and span around, trying to spot it, but all she could see was more smoke, getting thicker all the time. It was also getting hotter. Her back prickled and sweat began to gather on her forehead, under her arms. In her growing panic, she looked down at her hands, half-expecting them to be charred black and dripping with rendered fat. "A fire in the woods."

Although the crackling grew louder all the time, she couldn't see any flames. Alizon gathered up the hem of her tattered dress and pressed it over her mouth and nose. The animals around her were still fleeing in a panic, and with no other ideas, she tried to follow them. She stumbled once and fell to her knees, and for a long, panicky moment she could not get up again. Each scratchy, foul tasting breath seemed to shrink her lungs down to pebbles, and her head was throbbing again so painfully she thought that alone might strike her dead. But somehow she did find her feet, and she walked blindly on, the roar of the fire seemingly all around her.

I will be roasted after all, she thought. It was almost funny.

The heat was unbearable, and horrifically she could smell burning hair—the same arid, dry smell that sometimes filled the small house when their mother brushed her hair too close to the hearth and a stray strand of greyish-blonde hair curled and died in that impossible heat. Alizon coughed and fell again, finding herself at the base of an ash tree, its roots hard and hot under her hands. Desperate, she cringed against its wood and found a hole there in the ground, half-hidden and sheltered by the curling tree roots. She pulled herself down into it, ignoring how the sides of the hole scratched and pressed at her sides, and she passed down into the darkness of the underland and out of the reach of the fire.

Chapter Twelve

Beneath the forest, there were tunnels. Alizon had fallen onto the hard-packed earth, and she lay there for a time, trying to breathe the smoke back out of her lungs. Distantly, she could still hear the roar of the fire (or was it the beast?) but down here in the dark it was cool, and the ground beneath her was still. Gradually it became obvious that the place wasn't entirely dark after all; cracks in the ceiling of the tunnel were letting in a soft, yellow light, and as her eyes adjusted she found that it was more than enough to see by. Although it did trouble her, that light. If she were seeing daylight, what had happened to the fire? The hole that had led her down here was above her head somewhere, out of reach. The smell of smoke was still thick on her clothes and hair.

When she stood up, she found that the tunnel was just a little too small for her to walk upright. Instead she scurried forward, slightly bent. She would have to find another way out. Perhaps it would lead her closer to Dyersbrook. She had been lucky so far—so lucky—perhaps her luck would grant her one more boon.

Alizon had not quite been able to bring herself to leave Joan behind, so she had returned to her old ways. She walked in the woods and spoke to the faeries, leaving them offerings in likely places. A thimble of milk under an ash tree, a saucer of scrumpy under the stunted old apple tree at the edge of the village. She scavenged pieces of bright thread and made tiny, colourful dolls out of straw that she left perched in branches and at the edge of streams, or left atop old cairns. And all the time she would whisper to the fae: *protect her, protect my little sister, she is all I have left.*

Once, when she had been suffering her courses, she had taken a bloody rag deep into the woods at night, moving quickly with her heart thundering in her chest. She had buried it at the foot of a young sapling. *Let my blood feed your roots. I have given you everything.* The memory of it made her blush.

Once, she had taken the farmer Henry's son out into the same forest at night, and lay down on the black earth for him. As the boy had panted into her neck and spent himself, she had looked up at the branches above them. *I have given you everything, my queen.*

After walking a short way, she saw that there was something lying on the floor of the tunnel ahead of her. When she got closer she was not entirely surprised to see that it was John Bowman's head. His skin looked waxy and white, and the stump of his neck was ragged and torn. One dry eyeball rolled slowly in her direction.

"You," she said. "How did you get down here?"

"Beasts bury their food, don't they." His voice was raspy and slurred. Alizon could see the muscles in his face twitching as he forced the words out. "*You* should know that."

"The creature comes down here?" She had thought herself safe down in the underland.

"It goes wherever it likes, that thing."

Alizon crouched down next to the severed head. She reached out and pinched the skin of its cheek between her fingers and squeezed. It felt like touching old leather that had been rubbed with lard.

"What are you doing?"

"Does it hurt?" Alizon twisted the skin.

"You are an evil child. If the whole brood were like you, it is no wonder that your father could not bear the sight of his own family."

"What *I* wonder is whether men feel pain at all. You do love to inflict it, so surely you do not know what it is? You were going to burn me atop a hill, John Bowman."

"You killed your own father. Could there be a worse sin than that?"

"Yes. Oh yes." Alizon stood up again. "What is it, the creature? You must have seen it. The thing gnawed your head clean off."

John Bowman made a strange gurgling sound that Alizon eventually realised was laughter.

"Oh, you know what it is, girl. You know very well."

Grimacing slightly, she picked the head up by its hair and turned it over, so the thing was face-down in the dirt. Then she stepped over it and went on her way.

Chapter Thirteen

A LIZON WALKED THE TUNNELS FOR WHAT FELT like hours. She did not grow more hungry or more thirsty. She felt as though time had stopped in this hidden, secret place, and everything was held very still; she was a bee caught in treacle. Alizon imagined that she could walk the tunnels forever, and never age a day. She could come upon John Bowman's head years from now, and it would still be as fleshy, the blood on its ragged neck still wet.

Eventually, when she was sure she would be lost forever, Alizon saw a dim light in the distance. As she approached it she saw that there was a wall ahead of her, a simple wooden wall with a simple window, and the familiarity of it made her heart dance in her chest. It was their home, and through the window she could see their living room. Inside it, every one of her sisters.

There was Jenny, gone so long her face was almost that of a stranger. She was holding a baby in her arms—the baby had to be tiny Bethan, her face still red and birth-struck—and she looked happy, peaceful. Sat at the table were Meredith and Mary; Meredith had a piece of sewing in her lap, although she was ignoring that to glare at Mary, who was kicking her stockinged feet against the chair legs.

SEVEN DEAD SISTERS

Anne, Alizon's sweet little minnow, was curled in the chair their mother had always taken. She was eating a small green apple, her face scrunching up with the sourness of it. And Joan was sat just in front of her, on the threadbare rug in front of the fire. She was close enough to it to scorch, but then Joanie had always felt the cold. They were all together, but that was impossible.

Just then, Jenny looked up and caught sight of Alizon through the window. She waved her over, smiling.

"Alizon! There you are. We've been waiting for you."

She could no more have resisted that invitation than she could resist the beating of her own heart. Alizon went to them and climbed through the window into the living room. At once she was struck by the warmth of the place, and how good it felt to be there. Had it ever been this cosy in reality? Meredith got up from her place at the table and hugged her fiercely. Alizon bent to place a kiss on the top of her sister's head, and felt a strange light-headedness move through her. Meredith had been her big sister; not much older than her, true, but now she was ten forever and Alizon was a woman grown. With a start she realised she was older even than Jenny.

"What are you all doing here?" Her throat was dry as bark, so she tried again. "Why are you all under the ground?"

"Give her something to drink," Jenny said to Meredith, then turned her sunny face back to Alizon. "You've had a long journey, love. Rest with us a while."

Meredith went to the jug on the table and poured water into an old clay cup that Alizon recognised very well. She took it and held it, unable to stop looking at them all.

"I don't understand," she said eventually. "Not a thing that has happened to me today has made sense. I…" She trailed off. What day *was* it? How long had it been since she had eaten the poison Goodie had given her? How long had she been walking in the tunnels?

"Sit down," said Jenny. Her voice alone made Alizon feel strange.

So familiar and beloved, with every word spoken it seemed to uncover things she had forgotten, the very earliest artefacts of her childhood. "Anne, get up and let your sister sit in the good chair."

Anne scrambled up, giving Alizon a shy smile as she passed by. The girls all seemed at peace, content to be quietly sitting together in the small room.

"Where did you go, Jenny? When you left us."

Jenny smiled serenely, bouncing the baby gently on her knee. Bethan hiccupped.

"I planned to go to Dyersbrook, and then on from there to somewhere else. I don't think it really mattered where." She sounded wistful, as though remembering a distant sunny day. "I had scratched together a few coins that I thought might buy me passage on a cart going somewhere. South, I thought to go south. I wanted to see the sea. I had been saving food too, just tiny scraps really—a bit of hard cheese, some old bread. I thought I would mainly eat things from the forest, so I decided to leave that way rather than the road, which was a mistake. I left in the very middle of the night."

Alizon nodded. She had been no more than three when Jenny had vanished, but the day had left a mark on her anyway. Their mother had cried. Meredith had been quietly furious, in her way, and their father had left. "I'll bring her back," he had said, but he hadn't.

"I didn't get very far," Jenny continued. "These woods are strange, aren't they? And he knows them very well. You mustn't forget that, Alizon. Are you hungry, love?"

She was. Anne left the room (and where did that door lead, really? Were they still in the tunnels?) and returned with a steaming bowl held carefully in a kitchen rag. She gave the bowl to Alizon, and she looked down into it with a strange churning in her stomach. It appeared to be a kind of meat stew. She could see chunks of gristly-looking meat and small pieces of carrot.

"Eat up." Jenny turned to the rest of the girls. "Do you remember

Mother's stews? We didn't have them often, but when we did . . ." Alizon's sisters murmured with pleasure. Even Mary nodded, her big blue eyes filled with the good memory of hot food. "Those brief seasons of meat, they kept us going."

Alizon, a battered spoon in her hand, fished around in the stew, but did not move to eat it. Something about it made her deeply uneasy.

"I don't remember," she said quietly. "I'm not sure…"

"Oh, you must," piped up Joan. "Mother's stews were the best. We craved them all the time. We bothered her for them even when she was ill. You must remember that?"

Alizon put the spoon back down. Hearing Joan's voice, and seeing them all sitting together the way they were, their healthy faces shining, had reminded her of the last time she had seen them all together.

Chapter Fourteen

Joanie had thought she was safe, but Alizon had known better than that.

It was spring, and Alizon had been calling on an elderly neighbour who lived on the far side of the village. She did chores for the old woman in exchange for pennies, or skeins of wool from her rangy old sheep. That day it had been raining on and off, one of those ill-tempered spring days that promised a return of the sun's warmth but instead gave only a chill blue sky hidden behind racing clouds, and the occasional spatter of cold rain. Alizon made her way back, nodding to the few people she knew but mostly keeping her head down, and as she approached their own tiny house at the edge of the woods her stomach grew tight and strange. It became hard to breathe. She could see nothing untoward at their little curtained windows, yet even so the thought of going back inside there terrified her. Something was wrong.

Inside, her hands shaking, Alizon put the skeins of wool down on the kitchen table and listened very hard. The place was silent.

"Joanie? Joan, where are you?"

She went into the small kitchen area, which was gloomy and cramped, but the dark stains on the floor were clear enough. Stepping neatly across them, she threw the back door open and let the weak

SEVEN DEAD SISTERS

daylight in. There was blood on the floor, obscenely red and clearly freshly spilt.

"No…"

Alizon backed out into the garden. A lazy bee buzzed past her foot and she sprang away, skittish as a deer.

He's done it again, she thought, *only this time he has barely bothered to hide it. Now there are so few of us, why should he care? His neighbours have not raised an eyebrow as our numbers grew smaller and smaller, and I imagine he feels that no one is capable of striking him down.*

At the edge of their garden, he had been repairing the fence, and his old, sturdy mallet lay leaning against a post. She picked it up and headed out into the woods to look for him.

Anne took Alizon's arm and squeezed it.

'Where are you going?' she said, peering into Alizon's face. "You only just got here, will you not stay?"

Alizon drew away from her sister and put the bowl of meaty stew down on the table.

"You don't understand. This is all wrong."

It was not difficult to track her father. There were drips and splashes of blood all across the forest floor, spattered over leaves both living and dead. She could even smell it, a sharp mineral smell that made her heart pound. The forest itself felt strange, and gradually she realised it was deathly quiet—no birds were singing, and the constant shifting of the smallest beasts through the undergrowth had grown still. They could smell it too.

Eventually she came to a part of the forest she did not know, and that in itself frightened her because surely she had walked every inch of these woods since she was a child? Hadn't she sung and spoken and told stories to the fae here? Hadn't she left them cups of milk, piles of pennies, her own blood in a saucer or on a rag? How could there be a part of it that was hidden from her? But the answer was clear enough on all sides: this was his place, and she could only ever have found it by following the blood of her beloved sister.

Joanie is showing me the way, she thought. *A sister's blood speaks loudest to her sister.*

At first she took Joan to be the reflection in a puddle of water; the blank white clouds above mirrored on the forest floor. But as she approached she saw that those pale pieces were her sister's skin, the tangle around her, the torn tatters of her clothes.

"No."

Joan lay on her back, her arms out to either side and her palms face-up, as though she'd been trying to ward off some evil. Her face was white and waxy, her lips blue, and her eyes stared up at the sky. Already there were flecks of forest matter on her eyes, dusting them and taking away their sheen.

"No!"

Alizon went to her sister and tried to haul her up out of the debris, trying to shake the death out of her, but the girl was limp and lifeless, her body already beginning to grow stiff. With a moan growing in her chest, Alizon remembered how she had imagined Joan to be a changeling child, a creature carved from wood by the faeries and swapped for a real flesh and blood baby, and here she was, turning back into a mere bundle of pale sticks. Moving the body, Alizon saw a ring of dark bruises around the girl's neck, and she saw blood soaked into her drab, brown woollen dress. He'd throttled her, and stabbed her, and dragged her out here into the woods.

"Why? What for?" Alizon bit down a sob. "He's taken them all from me."

SEVEN DEAD SISTERS

She laid her sweet sister back on the dirt, and that was when she saw the other shapes lying beneath. Covered with a thin layer of black earth and the leafy mulch left over from winter, were five more sets of bones, lying neatly next to each other. It took less than a handful of moments to brush away the dirt, and there they were. Jenny, Meredith, Mary, Anne and even tiny Bethan. Who else could it be?

He had brought Joanie to join her sisters in their shallow graves.

—∽∼—

"That was the last time and only time I really saw you all together." Alizon looked at her sisters, who were watching her with a kind of gentle curiosity. "Don't you see? This is wrong. Jenny, you never met Mary, or Joan, or that baby you are holding. You were dead before they were born. None of this makes sense."

Alizon stood up from the chair. Abruptly, the room that had felt so cosy and safe a moment ago felt too small. The smell of dirt was overpowering. When she looked up, she saw not the battered boards that had made up the ceiling of their home, but a roof of hard packed earth, pocked here and there with dangling roots and pieces of old, black stone. The baby started crying.

"You're upsetting Bethan," Jenny said, mildly.

"This is..." Alizon looked at the window she had entered from, and saw smoke billowing in from the tunnel. As she watched it curled up to the dirt ceiling and began to roll towards where they all sat around the fire. "You can't stay here, the fire is coming. Come on, get up. We all have to leave, now."

None of the girls made to move. Anne sat down in the chair Alizon had left and drew her knees up to her chin. A distant roaring was growing closer.

"Come *on*." Alizon reached down to grab Meredith, who happened to be closest, but when her hand closed around the girl's chubby little arm she found herself holding old bones, their surface scratched with knife marks and gritty with black dirt.

"We can't go anywhere, love," Jenny said. "You know that don't you, Alizon dear?"

Alizon shook her head. Of all of it, it was the kindness in her sister's voice that hurt the most.

"And we can't go where *you're* going," added Anne. She peered at Alizon over the tops of her knees.

"Will you not come with me?" Alizon pressed the back of her hand to her mouth, hard, trying to push back the solid knot of grief that was constricting her throat. "Will you not?"

"Go," said Jenny. "And don't forget. He knows those woods too. And he's always hungry."

Chapter Fifteen

Back out in the tunnels, Alizon looked back. Their little home was still there, but through the window she could see fire engulfing their cosy living room. Flames ran up the dry old wooden walls, the rug by the fire was a carpet of heat, and amongst it all were her sisters. Sitting or standing, they were all aflame, their faces turned toward her, watching her go.

They were never there, she told herself. *You saw yourself where they are—a shallow grave in the darkest part of the forest, their bones clean and lying together.*

Picked clean.

She turned and ran, wanting to get away from the sight of their burning house, and the fire came on behind her, although sometimes it wasn't a fire at all but a beast, a beast that called out to her. The creature howled in her father's voice and what it said was:

I'm so hungry, Alizon. I must eat. You see that, don't you?

Alizon found her sisters in the wood but she did not find her father. Once she had covered the bones over again, she sat for a while with

Joan, one hand on her sister's cold cheek. She said some words over her, and more out of old habit than anything else, she took two of the pennies she had earned from the old woman and placed them on her sister's eyelids. Honeysuckle was growing nearby, so she picked some and left a ragged posy between Joan's fingers.

When she had done that, Alizon picked up her father's mallet again and made her way back through the woods. She felt as though she were drifting, and each footfall she made on the dirt path was numb and silent, as though she could not quite come into contact with the ground. All around her she sensed small things watching, their movements on the very edge of her sight, and so she sang to them under her breath. What did it matter now?

When she got back to their small house he wasn't there either, so Alizon walked back into the centre of the village. Some of her neighbours gave her curious glances—the heavy mallet at her side and the black dirt on her feet and hands made them wary, or perhaps it was just the expression on her face. *Yes, look,* she thought, her mind still drifting some way above her. *You should look. This is what you've wrought, all of you, for letting the Grey girls be taken into the woods.* She passed John Bowman, who was smoking a pipe by the well and pretending not to see her; she passed Thomas Whittle, who watched her very closely indeed, pausing in his work to straighten up and appraise her; she saw Goodie the wise woman, who shook her head and disappeared through a doorway out of sight. The day had turned brighter, warmer, and the scattered white petals of apple blossom blew across her path, like snow, or ash. She tightened her grip on the mallet. It did not feel heavy at all.

Alizon eventually found her father standing with some of the other men folk, discussing a horse that had become ill. The horse, a handsome chestnut coloured animal with a splash of white along his velvety nose, was standing near them, his head hanging low toward the ground, his flank spattered with white, foamy sweat. Some of the men turned to look at Alizon, their expressions either amused or irritated. Men folk rarely wanted girls listening to their conversations. Her father though, grinned widely. There were dots of blood on the cuffs of his shirt.

"There you are, girl. What do you want?" When she didn't answer, his grin only grew wider. "There is a mess in the kitchen for you to clean up, if you've nothing else to do."

"Why?" she said.

He shrugged and turned away, sharing a laugh with the other men folk. Alizon took a breath, gathering her strength, and she swung the mallet at the side of her father's knee. There was a sharp popping sound, and he gave out a strangled yell, half-dropping to the floor. The shape of his leg within his trousers was wrong, like there was a huge, misshapen potato where his knee should be, but Alizon barely spared it a glance.

"Jenny," she whispered.

With him half-kneeling in front of her, she lifted the mallet up high, and then brought it crashing down on the top of her father's head. He yelled again, but the sound was bitten off. The top of his head caved in, a soft-boiled egg at breakfast-time, and blood poured down his face.

"Meredith."

Alizon was aware of the cries of the other men, and even felt one of them try to grab her arm, but then he dropped it as though her skin were heated iron. She lifted the mallet and brought it down again, onto the sodden mess that was her father's temple; more bone splintered. Skin burst like overripe fruit. When she lifted the mallet again, she saw sticky strings of hair and something like porridge sticking to the underside of it. She smiled.

"Anne."

"Girl…" The word dripped from his lips. "Girl…"

"Just one for each of your daughters, Father," she said. She was surprised he could still talk. "Hold steady now. This one is for Bethan."

This time Alizon brought the mallet across to strike the side of his face. It was a weaker blow, but it still knocked his jaw out of joint. *No more words from you*, she thought.

"Alizon Grey, has the devil taken you?"

Alizon recognised the voice of John Bowman, the priggish magistrate who liked to lord it over the rest of them, but she also noticed that his voice was some distance away. They did not want to come near her. That was good.

The fifth blow finally dropped her father to the ground, and he rolled over, facing up into the sunlight. His face was a mask of blood, and his arms and legs were moving weakly, as though he didn't know which way was up.

"That was for Mary. And this one, sweet Father, is for Joan. My Joanie."

His face crumpled under the force of the mallet, a sharp snap as his nose was obliterated by it. When she lifted it again, there was little of him left. One eye had burst with the pressure of the impact and was trickling down his cheek like muddy tears. His mouth hung wide on his unhinged jaw, baring all his teeth.

"What big teeth you have, Father. And this one. This one is for me."

The final blow chased away the last shreds of him, and he lay in the dirt, his head a bloody pulp. With it all of Alizon's strength seemed to drain away, and she leaned heavily on the mallet, black spots dancing in front of her eyes. Around her, the hubbub of the village was growing, and at the edges of her vision she could see them approaching her, hands held out to grab. Some of them had weapons, knives and pitchforks and clubs. Someone was screaming in the crowd, and that struck her as funny.

"I am done," she said, and let the mallet drop. "Do what you will."

This time when they grabbed her, they did not let her go.

Chapter Sixteen

IN THE TUNNELS OF THE UNDERLAND, THE HEAT AT Alizon's back was growing unbearable. The fire was present as a constant orange glow just beyond the last corner, and the hot smell of burning hair. Every breath was smoke-tainted, but she kept running all the same, blindly taking turn after turn. Although the tunnels were narrow, she could sense other things in there with her. Scuttling shapes just out of sight, their eyes sharp and unkind. If she turned to look, they vanished, and their laughter was like the delicate peal of tiny silver bells.

"This tunnel must lead out somewhere," she said. "Another part of the woods…"

But it was getting harder and harder to remember what the woods looked like, harder to remember the taste of clean forest air. Wasn't it more likely that she had been down here forever, and that she would remain here? Always a few steps ahead of the fire, always unable to draw a full breath, while the backs of her arms and legs slowly blistered with the heat. She knew that she was no longer alone, and the capering things that scuttled at her heels were growing closer and closer—close enough to touch, almost. She thought about how John

Bowman and Goodie Pipkin had spoken of hell, and a suffocating fear began to close around her heart.

And then, it was gone. The tunnels had been replaced by a huge, vaulted chamber, and it was filled with clear, yellow light, although Alizon could see no windows. Under her feet the floor shone gold, and bright green shoots forced their way up through the cracks. In the centre of the chamber was a throne of bleached bones, and in it sat the most beautiful woman Alizon had ever seen.

"There you are, child." The woman's voice was honey. Her face was long and sly, her eyes green as clover. Her skin was mottled yellow and red, like an early summer apple. There was a lazy threat in the way she sat. "Do you know who I am?"

"You are the Queen of the Faeries," said Alizon. It was a simple fact. She could be no one else. At the edges of the chamber Alizon could see shadowed shapes watching her closely, their sly smiles hidden behind long-fingered hands. The faery court. "Where did the fire go?"

"There can be no fire here. But that is not the question you came here to ask, is it?"

Alizon nodded. She supposed she should have been frightened, but instead she felt empty.

"Why did you not protect my sisters? I gave you everything I could, and you never helped me. What more could I have done?"

"Never helped you?" The Queen shifted in her seat, uncrossing her long legs to lean forward and fix Alizon with her green stare. "You lived, did you not? When all around you died, you lived."

"*Me?*" Alizon rocked back on her feet as if she had been struck. "I did not ask for me! I asked for my sisters' lives."

The Queen looked away and shrugged her narrow shoulders.

"What you ask for with your mouth and what you ask for with your heart can be two different things, Alizon Grey."

The laughter of the court fluttered around the chamber.

SEVEN DEAD SISTERS

"That is a *lie*."

"Is it?"

Alizon said nothing.

"You went hungry, but you never starved. We made sure of that. When a man develops a taste for something, it is the easiest thing in the world to make it so that this is all he thinks of. All those seasons of meat, Alizon, meat that came from nowhere. You must have wondered?"

Alizon thought of the dog that had killed the chickens and bitten her hand. She thought of her father, grabbing her sister's shoulder in the deep of the winter and leading her from the room.

"*What did you do?*"

"What did we do? What did *you* do, Alizon Grey? You asked us for a boon and so, you went hungry, but you never starved. Your father was hungry too, but again and again his eye passed over you. You grew up safe and tall and strong, in the shadow of a monster we hid you from."

Alizon swallowed. She thought of Joanie's hands, speckled with blood, a wreath of honeysuckle pressed between them. "I never…I never asked for that."

"You like to pretend that you did not know, but when your mother grew ill and you pressed a pillow to her face, was your heart filled only with pity, or was there some other, darker passenger there? Some other passenger who knew who prepared and salted the meat, who made the stew and dished it up? Remember, Alizon, I have known every beat of your heart."

For a long moment Alizon said nothing. She was thinking of how John Bowman had pretended not to know Mary. How he had dismissed their horrors as "discipline".

"I have known many terrible things," she said eventually. "More than anyone should know. And almost the worst of it was how my neighbours pretended not to see. *That* is evil. Not a merciful pillow and a quick end."

"Were you angry with your father for killing Joan, or angry because there would be no more meat?" The Queen's lips parted in a wide grin, and all of her teeth were sharp. "Was your father the only one to develop a taste for it?"

"You are a liar." The words felt tired and colourless. "Everyone knows that about the faeries. You lie with every breath."

"Do I?" The Queen leant back on her throne, apparently satisfied. "And does it really matter? You have two choices now, Alizon Grey. You can stay in the underland and live your eternity in this place between places. There will be honey wine and fruit and, yes, meat. As much as you can ever eat."

From all around there was a whispering sound, and Alizon sensed the creatures watching from the walls baring their own teeth at her, their faces as sharp and as intent as the Queen's. They were hungry too, she realised.

"Or you go back up into the world and face the beast," continued the Queen. "Which will it be, little Grey girl?"

Chapter Seventeen

Up above ground, the sun was going down, and the woods were lit with the strange orange and purple lights of dusk. The fire was gone, and the trees were still. Alizon stood in a small clearing, glad to smell the good fresh scents of the forest. A cool breeze raised goose bumps on her arms and she shivered. In front of her, the beast crouched, a thing that was both her father and not him at all. Its yellow eyes rolled up to face her.

"Have you come to ask forgiveness, girl?" His voice was a growl and a gargle in a broken throat. "Have you come to say sorry for what you did? You ate the meat too. You thrived on their blood as much as I did, only you kept that knowledge from yourself—a mercy I was not granted."

As if to remind her, a flap of torn skin slowly unpeeled itself, revealing the ruined mess inside her father's head.

"Sorry?" Alizon laughed, and somewhere above her head the noise startled a bird into flight. She thought of her sisters, all six of them lying in the cold, dark earth. The mallet, somehow, was in her hands again, and she hefted the weight of it gratefully. "Ask forgiveness from you? Never. You should have been stronger than me, Father.

You should have stood against what was in your heart. But you couldn't. And in the end, neither can I."

The mallet was heavy, but, she noticed, not too heavy. She lifted it high above her head again.

"I'll need to eat if I'm to get to the next village."

Alizon Grey woke up on the killing road. She was weak and her hands shook dreadfully as she got to her feet, but lying on the road next to her was a package of carefully wrapped meat—fresh and red and dripping—and a leather bottle full of water. She picked them both up, and began the long, slow walk to Dyersbrook.